School Is A Nightmare #4

Yuck Mouth and the Thanksgiving Miracle

RAYMOND BEAN

www.raymondbean.com

Raymond Bean books

Sweet Farts Series

Sweet Farts #1
Sweet Farts #2 Rippin' It Old School
Sweet Farts #3 Blown Away

School Is A Nightmare Series

School Is A Nightmare #1
First Week, Worst Week
School Is A Nightmare #2 The Field Trip
School Is A Nightmare #3 Shocktober
School Is A Nightmare #4 Yuck Mouth and the
Thanksgiving Miracle
School Is A Nightmare #5
(Coming Winter 2013)

For Stacy, Ethan, and Chloe

Interested in scheduling an
author visit or web based author talk?
Email us at raymondbeanbooks@gmail.com

Contents

1
The Silent Treatment

Thanksgiving is kind of a non-holiday. You get a few days off from school, which is awesome, but there's nothing really special about it. Everyone eats turkey, which is kind of gross for me because I don't like it. A lot of people get all excited about pigging out on pie on Thanksgiving, but eating pie isn't really holiday-level excitement for me because my mom and sisters are basically addicted to pies. In the fall, we go through about two a week.

I was feeling pretty bummed out because I'd been looking forward to Halloween all of October, and then it was pretty much my worst Halloween ever. When I went to school on the day after Halloween, the kids in my class were still mad at me for a bunch of stuff that had happened.

It's a long story, but basically, our class pet, Myrtle the mouse, escaped a few weeks before Halloween. I took her out of the tank on a dare from this kid Cameron and dropped her by mistake. Before I could grab her and put her back in the tank, she scurried off and hid. If that wasn't bad enough, Myrtle was pregnant! She was missing for weeks, and by the time we caught her, she'd already had her babies.

The weekend before Halloween, my teacher, Mrs. Cliff, let me take Myrtle and her four babies home for the weekend. Unfortunately, my boa constrictor, Mr. Squeeze, got out of his tank and ate one of Myrtle's baby mice, the one named Calamity. It was a total accident. My friend Aaron and I were having a sleepover and left Mr. Squeeze out of his cage overnight. When we woke in the morning, Calamity was gone. I'm just thankful Mr. Squeeze didn't eat all of the mice. By the time Halloween rolled around, kids were looking at me as if I were a Halloween monster.

My classmates were definitely giving me the silent treatment because when I asked May, who sits right behind me, to borrow a pencil, she kept on working like she hadn't heard me.

Her friend Karen, who sits next to her, said, "Do you hear something?"

"No," May said. "I don't hear anything at all."

"Come on, guys," I said. "You're going to ignore me like I'm not even here?"

"Justin!" Mrs. Cliff said sternly. "After the drama that's taken place this week, I shouldn't hear a peep out of you."

"It's just that I don't have a pencil and the girls are totally ignoring me."

Mrs. Cliff handed me a pencil and sat down. The mouse tank was on the small table next to her desk. I couldn't help thinking about the other mice that were still loose in the classroom. I read online that mice usually give birth to about twelve babies. We'd found four babies, which meant there were about eight more baby mice hiding around our classroom.

I raised my hand.

"Yes, Justin?" Mrs. Cliff asked.

"Can we try to catch the other mice?"

"The custodians and I have been putting out safe traps every night since they went missing, and we've only caught a few."

"I know. Maybe the safe traps aren't working so well. We're studying mammals, right?"

"Yes…?"

"What if the class broke up into groups and studied the behavior of mice and each group worked on a different way to try and capture the mice safely?"

I think Mrs. Cliff was as surprised as I was about my suggestion.

"That's a good idea," May said.

"I'd love to do something like that," Karen said, purposely not looking at me. "Mice totally gross me out, but the thought of those poor babies roaming around in here at night all lost and hungry makes me really sad."

I could tell Mrs. Cliff was thinking about it. She walked slowly up my aisle and then down the next. The entire class watched her every move. I didn't think she'd agree because she usually doesn't want to hear what I have to say.

"Fine," she said without even looking at us. "It's a good idea and a good way to help the class heal from the loss of poor, helpless Calamity. We'll start tomorrow."

I couldn't believe she'd listened to my idea. I'd been pretty sure she'd treat me like garbage for the rest of the year after the mouse fiasco, but suddenly there was hope. I figured that if we could find the rest of those babies and Myrtle, she'd forgive me for what happened to Calamity.

2
Yuck Mouth

"**W**hat do you mean you're going to work in groups to find the mice?" Mom asked at dinner that night.

"Isn't that unsanitary?" my sister Becky asked.

"It's not like we're going to kiss them or anything. We're going to create safe traps to catch them and make sure they're safe."

"I don't know," Mom said. "It seems like everything you get involved with this year at school turns into a disaster. Why not just let the custodians and Mrs. Cliff deal with the mouse problem?"

"I don't think they should even let the kids stay in that class," said my other sister, Mindy. "There's probably mouse poop all over the place in there. It's gross."

"They're tiny little mice. It's not like we have eight hogs roaming around the place," I said.

"It's still gross," Becky insisted.

"Well, that's another reason for us to catch them," I said.

"What's your idea?" my dad asked.

"I don't know yet. I'm going to go on the Internet later on and see what mice like to eat and start with that."

"Why don't you just bring your snakes to class and let them slither around and eat the rest of the mice?" Mindy asked.

"That's not nice," Mom said. "Your brother feels terrible about the fact that Calamity was eaten by his snake."

"He feeds mice to his snakes all the time," Becky said. "He doesn't care that much. He just wants to get back on Mrs. Cliff's good side."

"Mrs. Cliff doesn't have a good side," I said.

Mom looked really angry. "You know, Justin, just when I thought you were making a change and taking things seriously, you have to go and say something like that."

"It's true. She's really mean and totally doesn't like me."

"I don't think she's that mean, but I completely get why she doesn't like you," Mindy said sarcastically.

Mom and Dad weren't in the mood for my sisters and me, I guess, because they sent us all to bed early. Becky complained that she hadn't done anything, but they didn't seem to care.

"Thanksgiving is in a few weeks, and you kids need to think a little more about how thankful you should be and quit all the arguing!" Dad said.

"And we're going to have company this year, so you guys better start working on your best behavior," Mom added. "I don't want to tell you what to do the entire time your cousin is here."

The girls smiled because they knew Mom was talking about my cousin Darwin "Yuck Mouth" McGee. Darwin lives in Florida, and I'd met him only one other time in my life, but Mom acted like we were best friends. The only thing I remembered about Darwin was his mouth. He once bragged to me about how he doesn't brush his teeth, *ever*! I believed him, too, because the night he slept in my room, his mouth smelled so bad I had to sleep with the covers over my head to keep the stink out. My sisters named him Yuck Mouth.

"Does anyone know if Darwin's started experimenting with brushing his teeth?" I asked.

"Go to your room, Justin," Mom ordered.

I didn't mind being sent to my room one bit. I didn't like the fact that Mom and Dad were mad, but I loved having a break from my sisters.

In my room, I put Mr. Squeeze over my shoulders and went online to figure out how to make the perfect mousetrap.

3
Scan It

The next day was Friday, and I had to go shopping after school with Mom and the girls for Thanksgiving supplies.

"How come we're shopping so early for Thanksgiving?" I asked. "Halloween was only two days ago."

"If you wait too long to get stuff for the next holiday, everything will be gone," Becky said. "Isn't that right, Mom?"

"It's true. I want to be ready for Thanksgiving. We're having it at our house this year, and if I don't start planning now, I'll be way behind."

The supermarket was jammed with people rushing around the store, buying everything they'd need for Thanksgiving. I was completely bummed that I was in the supermarket on a Friday night. There were about a zillion other things I'd rather be doing.

The only cool part was that Mom let me use the price gun for the groceries. We usually get all our stuff and then get up to the counter and pay the old-fashioned way, but the supermarket has these scanner guns where you scan the bar code on whatever you want to buy and it tallies it up for you. When you check out, all you have to do is hand the gun to the cashier, and out the door you go. I love anything that cuts down on time in the store, and I loved the scanner.

I was so bored I created a game where I tried to guess the price of an object and then scanned it to see how close I was. Each time after I scanned something, I deleted it from the order so we weren't charged. I was getting pretty good at it. I even guessed the price of a couple of things exactly.

"Why does everything end with ninety-nine cents?" I asked Mom.

"What do you mean?" she said, flipping over a turkey on a quest for the perfect one.

"Everything is priced two ninety-nine, three ninety-nine, twelve ninety-nine—you know what I mean. Why can't stuff just be an even number, like two dollars?"

"You're a weirdo," Mindy said.

I tried to scan her forehead with the scanner. "Stay still so I can scan your bar code."

"Mom! Justin's scanning my head."

Mom was elbow-deep in turkeys. About five other moms and a grandpa-looking guy all flipped and flopped the turkeys over, reading the weight and price as if they were looking for some hidden clue. *They need to get a clue*, I thought.

Mom didn't look up. She was in the zone. "Will you two please stop? This is important," she ordered.

I held the scanner up to Mindy's head again and pretended to read the price. "It says here that the item scanned is rotten."

"Cut it out!" Mindy growled.

"Leave her alone," Becky said, pinching me on the arm.

"Ouch! You two both belong on the rotten rack." I pointed to the discounted rack of old fruit and veggies. I scanned Becky's shoulder. "Yours says you expired about a month ago. Off to the Dumpster you go." I pretended to pick her up and carry her away.

"Stop it!" she demanded.

"Isn't it enough that you spoiled Halloween? Now you're going to spoil Thanksgiving too?" Mindy asked.

"I didn't spoil Halloween! I had a string of bad luck. And I don't know how you ruin

Thanksgiving. It's already one of the lamer holidays, if you ask me."

"Mom, Justin said Thanksgiving is lame," Becky tattled.

Mom finally surfaced with what she must have felt was the best turkey in the bunch because she was beaming with pride. You would have thought she'd tracked it in the wild and killed it herself.

"Here it is!" she exclaimed. "It's perfect—not too big, not too small. We'll have leftovers, but not so much that we can't eat it."

"Great job, Mom," Becky said.

"Looks perfect!" Mindy added.

"Looks like a turkey," I said. They all looked at me as if I'd said the worst thing ever. "What? It does."

Mom shook her head and rolled the cart away from the meat section. The cart was already filled almost to the top, and we'd been in the store for over an hour. *We've got to be almost done,* I thought.

"Girls, can you go up to the front of the store and grab us another cart? This one is about full."

"Another cart!" I cried. "Are we inviting the entire town over?"

"Justin, Thanksgiving is a feast, and a feast takes planning and a lot of ingredients," Mom explained.

The girls skipped off toward the front of the store. I followed sadly behind Mom. It felt like we'd never get out. I imagined what it would be like if the supermarket had a game room where kids could play while their parents shopped for food.

4
Pay Up, Pilgrim

Mom filled the second cart over the next hour of shopping. By the time we got to the register, we'd been in the store for over two hours. It felt as if we'd climbed to the top of Everest. We stood before the cashier, and everyone looked at me.

"Justin, hand her the scanner," Mom said.

"You're all set," the clerk said. "If your Ultra Mega Market account is linked to your credit card, you can just click 'done,' put the scanner back on the charging wall, and you're all set."

I nodded approvingly. *That's how it's done,* I thought. If I'd been in charge of this mission from the beginning, we'd have been out of there a long time ago.

"Great thinking, Justin," Mom said. "That saves us some time."

It was the first time in a while that I felt like I wasn't getting in trouble. The girls didn't seem to like it very much. We jammed all the food into Mom's little Honda Civic and headed for home. There was so much stuff that grocery bags stuffed the trunk, filled the front passenger seat and the floor, and were on all of our laps. I was so thrilled to finally get out of the supermarket. I felt like I'd been released from some kind of hostage situation. The smell of all the food was making me hungry, and I hadn't had dinner yet.

When we were about halfway home, Mom's phone started ringing. She asked me to answer it and put it on speaker.

"Hello?" Mom said.

"Hey, it's me," Dad said.

"Dad, help!" I joked. "I'm trapped in the shopping trip that will never end!"

"Justin, I need to talk with your mom for a second. Honey, are you aware that you spent close to seven thousand dollars at the supermarket!"

"What are you talking about?" Mom asked, panicked.

"I just got a call from the credit card company to let me know we had a major purchase on our card that looked suspicious. How much food did you guys buy?"

Mindy and Becky looked at me and smirked.

"What?" I asked.

"I'll bet I know how Mom got seven thousand dollars charged to her card," Becky said.

"That was an expensive game of Guess the Price you played back there," Mindy added.

"What's Guess the Price?" Mom asked. "Please tell me you weren't playing with that scanner, Justin."

"I wish I could, Mom, but..."

"How many things did you scan?" she demanded.

"Everything he passed," Mindy said.

"I did not," I said. "I scanned a lot of things, but then I deleted them. Do you want to know how much cow intestines cost?"

"I'm sure I can find out when I check my receipt," Mom said, turning the car around. "We're going back."

"No!" I pleaded. "We've already been gone forever. Take the money out of my future earnings. I don't care how much it costs. Don't make us go back there!"

"What's a scanner?" Dad interrupted.

"I'll call you back," Mom said. "We're going back there!" Mom ignored me, of course. She was freaking out and had stopped listening to anything I said minutes before. It took us about ten minutes to get back to the parking lot.

"Where's the receipt?" Mom asked, pulling into a parking spot.

"I threw it out on the way out of the store," I said.

Mom fixed her hair in the rearview mirror. I tried to avoid eye contact. I could feel Becky and Mindy glaring at me from each side. There was nowhere to look, so I looked down at the floor. I felt like a dog that's in trouble and can't bring itself to look its master in the eye.

"Let's go," Mom said. "Hopefully they can fix this."

"We've been here for so long," I complained.

Mom ignored me and led the march back into the store. The girls followed behind her like baby ducks following their mother to the pond. I trailed behind, knowing we weren't going to get out of the store quickly.

Mom got in a big argument with the manager of the store when he suggested that if she'd kept an eye on her son—that's me—the situation wouldn't have happened.

He also said he had to charge her because we'd left the store and there was no way of proving that we didn't buy all the items on the receipt, take them home, and then come back to the store. He was basically calling Mom a liar, which was terrible to see. I even got involved and showed the guy what I'd been doing.

"Look," I said. "I scanned an item…" I looked around and decided to scan a *People* magazine. The scanner read $4.95. "And then I clicked this green button to delete it."

"That green button adds the item to your total," the manager said.

Mom was furious as we marched out of the store a half an hour later. She cried the whole way home, which made the girls cry too. I sat sandwiched between my sisters, wishing I had $7,000 to make it all stop. In that moment, I would have paid $100,000 for a little peace and quiet.

5
Thanksgiving = Honesty

Mom and Dad spent most of the weekend on the phone with the credit card company and the managers at the supermarket. They finally agreed to split the bill, which meant Mom and Dad had to pay about three thousand dollars for a Thanksgiving dinner that should have cost about three hundred.

Later that night, while I was watching TV, I heard Dad say in the kitchen, "We could have flown to the Caribbean for a week for the same price this Thanksgiving is costing us."

"I can't believe this is happening," Mom said. "We're never using those scanners again."

"Maybe next time Justin shouldn't go to the supermarket," he suggested.

"I didn't mean to do it," I called, but the idea of getting out of grocery shopping sounded pretty good to me.

I was grounded all weekend and bored out of my mind by the time Sunday night rolled around. I sat in my room thinking about all the people who were mad at me. The craziest part was that none of the things they were mad at me for were my fault. Mrs. Cliff was mad about the mice: not my fault. Becky and Mindy were mad because I'm smarter and more awesome than them: not my fault. Mom and Dad were mad about the $3,000 Thanksgiving dinner: not my fault.

That's when I remembered that Mrs. Cliff wanted us to make a list of all the things we were thankful for and turn it in at school on Monday. I got out my notebook and started my list.

Things I'm Thankful For
1. My snakes
2. My friend Aaron
3. Doritos
4. Xbox
5. Candy
6. Shorts
7. Gum
8. Ice cream
9. Sports
10. TV

I shared my list with the class on Monday morning. "What about your family?" Mrs. Cliff asked.

"I don't know," I said. "They're in my life, but I wouldn't say I'm thankful for them right now. My sisters treat me pretty bad, and my parents have grounded me for most of the last few weeks. I'm just being honest. Isn't that what Thanksgiving is all about, honesty?"

I knew what Mrs. Cliff was looking for. She wanted us to write lists saying how thankful we were for our parents, sisters, families, blah, blah, blah. The truth was that I wasn't feeling thankful for my family. I also knew Mrs. Cliff wasn't going to let me get away with the list I'd written, but I wasn't in the mood to give in.

"Justin, do you really think Thanksgiving is about honesty? After all the Thanksgiving lessons you've learned in first, second, and third grade, you honestly think it's about honesty?"

I had a feeling she knew I was messing with her.

"I do," I bluffed.

"Please, tell us how Thanksgiving is all about honesty," Mrs. Cliff encouraged.

It was clear she was messing with me, and she'd picked the wrong day because I had nothing to lose. I was already grounded, Mom and Dad were already super mad at me, and Mrs. Cliff was still holding a grudge from the mouse incidents.

"Thanksgiving is the holiday where we celebrate honesty because the Pilgrims stole the turkeys and all the land from the Native Americans. The Native Americans signed a contract saying they would let the Pilgrims stay on their land for a bunch of pots and stuff. Then the Pilgrims stole all the land and the Native Americans had to sell all their stuff and walk to Florida or something. Today we try to remember the importance of always being honest because of that first Thanksgiving in Florida."

The class fell completely silent. No one knew what to make of my confusing speech. I was signing my own death warrant. I understood that. Mrs. Cliff was set to explode, but she didn't. She called on someone else and ignored me. I knew it was some kind of knew stragegy she must have read about in one of her teacher magazines.

After asking a few other kids what Thanksgiving meant to them, she calmed a little and, "Thanksgiving isn't about honesty, Justin. But your indifference and misunderstanding of the holiday's true meaning is both alarming and inspirational. You've given me an idea. I think we should research the holiday and decide for ourselves what we think the true meaning of Thanksgiving is to each of us."

"No need," I said. "I think we'd all like to hear what the meaning of Thanksgiving is from you, Mrs. Cliff."

"That's the thing. There are some things I can't teach, Justin, and this is one of them. You kids are going to have to roll up your sleeves and find the true meaning of Thanksgiving for yourselves."

It felt like all the kids were giving me dirty looks. I think someone behind me may have even growled.

6
A Hundred Years

Mrs. Cliff handed out a sheet at the end of the day for us to complete at home. We each had to find ten new things about Thanksgiving for homework. When I got home, I went on the computer. I couldn't find anything that I didn't already know about Thanksgiving, so I made some things up. I put the paper back in my bag and played with my snakes.

Thankfully, I had them safely in their tanks when Mom walked into my room.

"What did I do now?" I asked.

"That's what I wanted to talk to you about," she said. "Mrs. Cliff just called to say you were being a bit difficult in class today. I feel like that's the way it's been around here lately. I don't understand why you've been getting in so much trouble. Is something bothering you?"

"Yes," I said.

"What is it?"

"School. I can't stand it. Mrs. Cliff is the worst. Can't you call the principal and tell her you want me moved to Mrs. Fiesta's class?"

"Mrs. Cliff is not the worst, and you need to take a long, hard look in the mirror, young man. You walk around blaming your mistakes on your teacher and your sisters, and I don't hear you taking any blame."

"I haven't done anything," I protested.

"Who let the class pet out of the tank last month?"

"Yeah, but…"

"No buts. Who let the mouse out of the tank?"

"Me."

"Whose snake ate the mouse when you took the tank home for the weekend?"

"Mine."

"And who scanned everything in the store at the supermarket and cost his mother and father thousands of dollars?"

"I get it," I said. "But I didn't mean any of those things. They just kind of happened. I don't want to be in trouble."

"Good. I don't think you want to be in trouble, but you need to start thinking about the things you do. Sometimes I honestly don't know what goes through your head."

"That makes two of us, but I'm telling you, Mrs. Cliff doesn't like me."

"Maybe she doesn't like the way you're behaving and the choices you're making. It's not you she doesn't like, it's what you're doing. Start behaving better, and you won't have as many issues with her."

"I'll try, but she definitely hates me," I said confidently.

Mom's phone buzzed, and she checked her e-mail. "Oh, it's Aunt Veronica. Darwin can't wait to come and spend some time with his best cousin. They'll be here on Sunday, November eighteenth."

"We have school until the twenty-first. Does that mean I don't have to go to school on the days they're here?"

"No, you have to go to school. It should be a lot of fun having them here. You haven't spent time with Darwin in a long time."

"I don't know him at all. We hung out once when I was little, and I haven't seen him since."

"You two are going to have a blast! I want you to promise me you won't give him a hard time about his breath and you won't say a word about how much money we spent for Thanksgiving. If your aunt knows what happened at the store, she'll feel terrible."

"I won't say anything about the money, but can you please make Darwin brush his teeth?"

"He brushes his teeth, Justin. He was only kidding when he told you he doesn't."

"I don't know. You didn't have to sleep with him. I could live to be a hundred years old, and I'll never forget that stench."

7
Gotcha

The next day in class, everyone shared their facts about Thanksgiving. I was thankful Mrs. Cliff didn't collect the lists because I hadn't written anything down that made any sense. I held my paper close to my chest so no one could see it.

Kids mentioned some things I never knew about Thanksgiving. Cameron said that the kids weren't allowed to sit during the meal at the first Thanksgiving and they had to stand while the adults ate. May shared that they didn't use utensils like forks, that they probably just used their hands or a shell to eat. Karen said she'd read online that people were very dirty in those days and would wipe their hands on long tablecloths.

Mrs. Cliff made a list on the easel. "This list is looking great. We'll keep it posted and add to it as we learn new things about Thanksgiving. Also, we are going to start planning today for our Thanksgiving feast on November twenty-first. I've decided that we'll have a great big feast and invite all of your parents and younger brothers and sisters to join us. This way it will give us a better feeling of what that first Thanksgiving might have felt like."

May raised her hand.

"Yes, May?" Mrs. Cliff asked.

"Can we dress up like Native Americans and Pilgrims?"

I was surprised by how many kids in the class seemed to want to dress up. I raised my hand, and Mrs. Cliff called on me.

"I think we're too old to get dressed up," I said.

"I love the idea," Mrs. Cliff said. "Let's put it to a vote."

The only two people to vote against dressing up were Howard Lofegh and me. After Howard saw that we were the only two voting against it, he changed his vote.

"All right, it's decided. We'll be dressing for our feast," Mrs. Cliff declared. "I think it would be a hoot to make our own costumes and make some for the parents as well."

The class cheered. I don't know what it was about me that didn't feel excited about dressing up, but I was clearly the only one. Everyone else thought it was the coolest thing ever.

Later in the day, we spent about an hour working on our mousetraps. My group's was actually pretty good. I was the most into it, and the group basically let me do what I wanted. I looked at a bunch of different safe traps online and decided on a setup where the mouse gets stuck in its own tank.

The plan was to use a yardstick and angle it so the mouse could climb up the stick and onto the top of its tank. I brought in a screen from one of my old cages and cut a hole in the top. The plan was to place a thin cloth over the hole and put a small piece of cheese in the middle of the cloth. If all went right, the mouse would walk up the yardstick, scurry across the screen, and go for the cheese. When it stepped onto the cloth, it would fall through the hole and be right back in the tank. My group loved my idea. They were pretty smart.

"That won't work," Karen said when we presented our idea to the class.

"Of course it will. It's perfect," I argued.

"Won't the mouse be able to just climb right back out the hole if it's foolish enough to fall in?"

"Nope, because the hole is in the middle of the screen. We'll take out anything that would allow the mouse to climb up on the sides and get back out of the hole."

"What if it breaks its neck falling through the hole?" May asked.

"What are you talking about? It's a mouse. They can fall from really high places and they're fine."

That's when I realized that May and Karen were trying to make my idea look bad because they wanted to win.

"I think it's a fine idea, Justin," Mrs. Cliff said. "Your group did a great job. It's nice to see you putting such effort into something."

A few other groups shared their ideas, which were pretty bad and probably wouldn't catch the hungriest mouse in the world with the last crumb on the planet. The only other trap that seemed like it might work was from Karen and May's group. They used a plastic container turned upside down. It was propped up on one side by a small stick. Attached to the stick was a string, and on the end of the string was a piece of fruit.

"The mouse will nibble on the fruit, and if he pulls on the string at all, the stick will fall over, and the whole container will trap the mouse inside," May explained.

"It won't work," I said.

"Why not?" Karen asked.

"Because it was your idea," I said.

"Justin, that's enough," Mrs. Cliff said, and made me apologize. "We will find out in the morning, won't we?"

She instructed everyone to set up the traps carefully before we packed up to go home for the day. Looking around the room, I was pretty confident we were going to win.

There were no mice in any of the traps until the end of the week. Then on Friday when we came in, there was a mouse in my trap, a mouse in Karen and May's trap, and one in the custodian's trap. I imagined all the mice running wild the night before, having a grand old time until they were snagged in our traps. I felt a little sorry for them, but Mrs. Cliff and the principal were super excited. That put the number of baby mice at seven, minus Calamity, of course.

Before we went home for the weekend, we set the traps again because we were pretty sure there were a few more babies running wild in the classroom. I really wanted to catch Myrtle since I was the one who let her loose in the first place.

8
No Justice

Saturday morning, Mom and I were eating breakfast, and she was looking through my backpack.

"Oh, you didn't tell me you're having a Thanksgiving feast at school."

"We just found out about it. Mrs. Cliff wants us and you to dress like Native Americans or Pilgrims."

"Which are we?"

"She's going to tell us on the day of the feast. I'm thinking I should probably stay home with my favorite cousin, Darwin."

Becky walked in and grabbed an apple from the fruit bowl. "You mean Cousin Yuck Mouth?"

"Becky, that's terrible!" Mom said.

I couldn't believe it—Becky was about to get in trouble instead of me for a change. I waited for Mom to hand out the punishment.

"That's it?" I asked.

"What do you mean?"

"I mean you're not going to punish her for calling Darwin 'Yuck Mouth'?"

"You were the one who came up with that name in the first place," Mindy said, walking in and opening the fridge.

"Justin!" Mom exclaimed. "How could you use such a terrible nickname for your lovely cousin Darwin?"

"I didn't even say anything. I might have called him that a long time ago."

"You still do," Becky said.

I couldn't believe how much the girls got away with. They did and said whatever they wanted.

Calling Darwin "Yuck Mouth" was the perfect example. Becky had been the one to call him that, but because I had once said it a few years before, I was in trouble.

9
Where's the Pool?

The following week flew by. I didn't get in any trouble, which was nice for a change. We didn't catch any mice, which was frustrating, and my cousin Darwin arrived on the Sunday before Thanksgiving as planned.

Before we answered the door, Mom got us all together and said, "Please do not embarrass me and say something insensitive about Darwin. I'm sure whatever breath issues he had years ago are resolved by now."

She opened the door. Aunt Vanessa and Darwin were standing on our porch with their suitcases. Darwin had on swimming goggles with a snorkel attached to the side. Aunt Vanessa had a huge rolling suitcase. Darwin was holding a plastic grocery bag bulging with stuff.

"Hi!" Mom said. "Come in, you two."

Darwin looked pretty much the same as I remembered him. He was taller than me, with messy hair. He looked like he was good at sports.

"Can I go swimming?" he asked before even saying hello to all of us.

"We don't have a pool," I said.

"You boys can play outside," Mom said.

"I don't think so," Darwin said. "Mom told me you guys had a pool."

"Why'd you tell the boy that?" Mom asked my aunt Vanessa.

"It was the only way to get him here. He would have complained the entire way otherwise."

"It's November," I said. "This is New York. It gets pretty cold up here. Even if we had a pool, it's too cold to go in anyway."

"Darwin isn't the best in geography," Aunt Vanessa said.

"You didn't know that it gets cold in November in New York?" Becky asked.

"Becky," Mom warned. "Why don't you help show Aunt Vanessa to the guest room, and Justin can show Darwin to his room."

"He's staying with me?" I asked, surprised.

"Yes, Justin. It will be like a sleepover party."

"I hope you like snakes," I said. "Because I have two of the coolest snakes in the world."

"I live in Florida. We have snakes that can kill you in our backyard," Darwin said.

"That's awesome!"

"You have a snake in the house?" Aunt Vanessa asked, sounding concerned.

"I have two," I said.

"Take Darwin to your room," Mom directed. "The girls and I will get Aunt Vanessa settled in.

Darwin, we're so happy you and your mom are here to join us for Thanksgiving." She reached out to give him a hug.

He leaned in to hug her back and said, "It's good to be here. You guys are the only cousins I have."

When he said it, Mom must have gotten a whiff of his breath, because she looked like she'd just opened the door to a barn full of manure on a hot day.

"Oh my," she said.

"What is it, Mom?" I asked, grinning. The girls were grinning too.

"I'm so happy to have your cousin here at last," she said, turning her head away from him and pretending to cough in her arm. "Take him up to your room now."

"Is that a tear in your eye?" I asked.

"I'm just feeling sentimental," Mom said, wiping at her face.

10
Eat It

When we got to my room, Darwin plopped his stuff down on my bed and said, "What do you want to do?"

"We could go in the woods and look for snakes and stuff," I suggested.

"Cool." We walked out the back door and followed the trail into the woods. "This is pretty cool," he said. "Are there any alligators?"

"No, we don't have alligators in New York. It's pretty cold this time of year, so I don't usually find much back here. But in the summer, I find all kinds of cool critters."

"Where I live, it's warm all the time. There's a swamp behind our house, and we have a couple of alligators in it."

"That's awesome. Do you ever see them?"

"Yeah, check it out," he said, holding out his phone to show me the pictures of the alligators. "You should come visit us sometime. It's pretty cool where we live. We've got real snakes that can kill you. You'd love it."

We flipped over a bunch of rocks and climbed a few trees, but didn't find anything cool. Justin saw a chipmunk, and we chased a few squirrels. We were high in a tree when we heard it.

"What was that?" Darwin asked. We were about twenty feet up, and something on the ground made a noise like bubbling water.

"I don't know," I admitted, wondering what could have made the noise.

"Maybe it's Bigfoot," Darwin said.

I laughed because I thought he was kidding, but from the look on his face, he was being serious. "There's no such thing as Bigfoot," I said.

"Yeah, there is. I've seen her."

"You've seen Bigfoot? And it's a girl?"

"Yep," he said. "I was out one morning looking for lizards when—"

"Stop," I interrupted, pointing to a large patch of tall grass and bushes. "Look."

"What is that?" he asked.

"I think it's a turkey."

We sat there staring at it for a few minutes, when he finally said, "Let's get it."

I nodded.

We slowly lowered ourselves out of the tree and walked carefully toward the turkey. It was huge and had loads of feathers. It was facing away from us and didn't hear us coming until we were right near it. Darwin made a lunge for it and missed. The turkey took off running through the bushes. We ran after it and tried our best to keep up.

We must have chased that turkey for two hours before it got so tired it simply let us pick it up. Darwin grabbed it from behind and wrapped his arms around the wings.

"What do we do with it?" he asked.

"Let's take it back to my house. We'll eat it for Thanksgiving."

"Awesome!"

We slowly made our way back out of the woods and to my backyard. The girls were playing soccer, and Mom and Aunt Vanessa were sitting at the patio table. I thought Aunt Vanessa was going to fall down when she saw her son holding a massive turkey.

"Get a rope!" Darwin ordered, struggling to carry the turkey. The girls screamed and ran into the house, leaving the back door open. Mom and Aunt Vanessa both shouted for Darwin to put the turkey down.

"We need a cage or some kind of rope," I said. "Hold on to it while I go grab something."

"Hurry," Darwin said. "I'm losing my grip."

I sprinted to the garage, where Mom kept an old toddler corral from when I was little. Dad had been telling her to throw it out for years, but she liked to keep it around in case anyone ever came by with a little kid. I threw the pieces in the wheelbarrow and raced around to where Darwin had the turkey.

I quickly linked the pieces of the corral together and created a pen for the turkey. The whole time Mom and Aunt Vanessa were talking a mile a minute. I was so excited I could hardly hear what they were saying. When the corral was ready, Darwin dropped the turkey in and gave me a high five. Then I noticed that blood was dripping from his cheek and one of his legs.

"That was awesome!" he shouted.

"I know!" I said.

"Justin!" Mom cried.

"What?"

"Don't you realize our yard is fenced? We've been trying to tell you that you don't need the kiddie corral."

I laughed. "I didn't even hear you saying that. We were so focused on it getting away."

"You might as well leave it," Darwin said. "He seems to like it."

"What in the world is that thing?" Aunt Vanessa asked.

"It's a wild turkey," I said. "We're going to eat it on Thanksgiving."

11
Turkey Heroes

After about half an hour of our convincing my mom and Googling how to take care of a turkey, Mom and Aunt Vanessa agreed to let us keep the bird for a few days if we agreed to release him on Thanksgiving. We said we would.

"You're really going to let them keep this gigantic bird in the backyard?" Becky asked Mom.

"I'm not thrilled about the idea, but look how much fun they're having. If they let it go on Thanksgiving, I don't see the harm."

"Besides," I said, "while the rest of the world is eating turkeys, we'll be setting one free."

"Yeah," Darwin said. "It's like we're turkey heroes or something."

By the time we came in and took showers, it was after ten. We had spent the entire day outside with the turkey. Darwin and I were watching TV in my room when he said, "I think I have something in my hair."

I knew immediately it was a tick. "Mom!" I shouted. "You might want to come up here."

The woods behind my house were loaded with ticks. My dad said that when he was a kid, there weren't any ticks. I usually stayed on paths and out of the bushes and tall grass, so I rarely got them, but we were running through all of it when we chased the turkey. If Darwin had one, I knew I probably had a few more.

Mom and Aunt Vanessa picked over us like mama chimpanzees looking for bugs. I had three ticks, and Darwin had six! It was so gross. After Mom plucked them off of us, she made us each take a bath and then a shower to be sure they were all gone.

When we finally got to bed around midnight, I was exhausted. I lay in my bed, and Darwin was on the floor with his sleeping bag. I had on a dust mask I'd found in the garage to help protect against the smell of his yuck mouth. He was already just about asleep. The turkey gobbled outside.

"Sorry about the ticks," I said through my mask.

"Totally worth it," he mumbled, and fell asleep.

I rolled over to face away from him. He was right. It was totally worth it.

12
The Worst
Case of Poison Ivy Ever

I woke up first the next morning. It was Monday, and I totally didn't want to go to school. I looked out my window and saw the turkey out in his pen, gobbling away. I went online and Googled what I should feed him. It said they eat just about anything, including snakes, which is not cool. They love acorns and will eat birdseed.

I ran downstairs and went out to the shed, where Dad keeps the birdseed. I threw a handful of seed into the pen and gathered up a bunch of acorns from under the big trees in the front yard. In the fall, our lawn is covered with acorns, so that was easy enough. Then I went inside to wake up Darwin. When I got to my room, he was still sleeping, but I noticed something I hadn't seen when I first woke up. His face was completely swollen and covered in a poison ivy rash. I looked a little closer and saw that it was on his hands too.

"Darwin," I whispered, pinching my nose. "Wake up, buddy. I think you may have a touch of poison ivy."

"Huh?" he mumbled, starting to come out of it.

"Looks like you have a little case of the itchies there, pal." I was trying to make it sound as if it wasn't a big deal, but he was in trouble.

He sat up and immediately started scratching his face.

"Take it easy," I said. "You don't want to pop those blisters." It was easily the worst case of poison ivy I'd ever seen, and I'd had it pretty bad before. The poison ivy that grows in the woods behind my house is super strong. Even when the trees drop their leaves for the season, the poison ivy vines and dead leaves are still dangerous. Our neighbor gets it every year when he rakes his leaves.

He stood up and walked toward the mirror. I could see that it was all up his arms and on his legs too.

"I think you might have a little poison ivy," I said.

He took one look in the mirror and shrieked loud enough that everyone in the house woke up. They ran into my room one after the other. Each of them reacted the same way. It was as though Darwin had mutated overnight. Mom got the doctor on the phone, and Dad looked through the medicine cabinet for some poison ivy cream, even though all the cream in the world wouldn't help the rash Darwin was dealing with. The girls looked as if they might get sick.

"Is it that bad?" Darwin asked Mindy.

"Yeah," she said. "It's, like, the worst case of poison ivy ever!"

I had to give it to Mindy. She was honest.

"Don't say that to him," Aunt Vanessa said.

"It's true," Becky exclaimed. "Would you rather we tell him he's fine? Look at him! His head looks like a brain!"

"You're going to be fine," I reassured him. "I've had poison ivy so many times. It will be gone in a few days."

"Did you ever have it this bad?" he asked.

No, I thought, *no one's ever had it that bad.*

13
Wonderful

Dad loaded the girls and me into his car and drove us to school, and Mom and Aunt Vanessa took Darwin to the doctor. I was pretty exhausted from being up so late the night before and all the poison ivy drama in the morning. I'd forgotten all about our Thanksgiving feast on Tuesday.

We spent most of the day finishing up our costumes for the parents to come in for the feast. Mrs. Cliff explained that the Pilgrims didn't have enough tables and chairs so they used whatever they had, like barrels, planks of wood, and tree stumps, to eat on. She explained that the Pilgrims didn't have sugar or ovens at the first Thanksgiving, so there were no pies. She went on to say that they didn't even have forks, so most of the eating was done with their hands.

"Can we eat that way?" I asked, figuring she'd get mad at me.

"Yes, Justin. We'll try our best to re-create the feast of the first Thanksgiving. And to really make the experience authentic, we'll eat outside. Several parents are helping with the cooking and following recipes I gave them using only ingredients that would have been available at the time of the first Thanksgiving."

Out of the corner of my eye, I noticed a small figure scurry across the floor. I got up and lunged at it. It felt warm and furry in my hand. "I did it!" I cried. "I got another mouse!"

Mrs. Cliff tried to fake a smile. "Wonderful."

14
His Mouth Died, and His Body Kept On Living

When I got home, Mom told me that Darwin wasn't feeling very well. The doctor had had to give him a shot for the poison ivy to try to stop it from spreading. I went upstairs to my room and found him lying in my bed, sleeping. I wasn't too thrilled about him being in my bed with the worst case of poison ivy the world has ever seen.

I went back downstairs. "Mom, I don't want to come off mean or insensitive, but is it such a good idea for Darwin to be in my bed with all that poison ivy?"

"The doctor said it's fine. He said as long as I wash the sheets before you go back in them, you'll be fine."

"Still, it's kind of gross."

Mom was pretty angry. "I think you're being kind of selfish. Imagine you were down in Florida and you got poison ivy. I'll bet Darwin would let you use his bed."

"I wouldn't ask to sleep in someone else's bed if I was covered in poison ivy. I'd sleep on a couch or in a sleeping bag or something, but not in someone's bed. What if I get it?"

"We're done talking about this," Mom said.

I walked back up to my room and checked on the snakes. Then I clicked on the TV and sat in the chair at my desk. I was watching *Sports Recap* on the baseball channel when I smelled it. I would know that smell anywhere: Darwin's breath. *Yuck Mouth!* I thought. I turned on my fan, even though it was pretty cold outside, and grabbed a bottle of room freshener from the bathroom and sprayed it around. It didn't help. I could still smell the yuck.

I walked to Becky's room. She was on the computer, and Mindy was working on her homework. "Hey, guys, Darwin is in my bed, and he's covered in poison ivy."

"We know," Mindy said. "We saw. That's not cool."

"Thank you! Mom acted like I was being difficult because I didn't want him in my bed. I'll bet she wouldn't want him in her bed either. He's been closed up in there all day and night, and his breath is unbelievable! It's like his mouth died and the rest of his body kept on living."

"It can't be that bad," Becky said.

"It's worse," I assured her.

My dad appeared at the door. "Hey, Justin, your turkey is gobbling like crazy out there. Are you really planning on keeping him until Thanksgiving?"

"It's going to be a cool thing on Thanksgiving, Dad. Also, I'm protecting him, because if someone finds him between today and Thanksgiving, they might want to eat him. I'm kind of a turkey hero."

"You're ridiculous, but you're not a hero," Becky said.

"Can't I be both?" I said.

"Whatever you are, there's a gobbling turkey in our yard that needs your attention," Dad said.

I walked outside and gave the turkey some more seed and water. I threw a few more acorns in for him. He looked at me and gobbled.

"Hang in there, big fella. I know you want to get out of here, but it's too dangerous. If I let you go now, there's a good chance you'll end up on someone's dinner table. I'm not going to let that happen."

I hung out with the turkey for a while and then went in to check on Darwin. He was in a lot of pain and super itchy. His mom said he hadn't eaten anything all day. I slept on the couch that night because between Darwin's breath, the scratching, and the moaning from the itching, I felt like I was in the zoo.

15
You Haven't
Been That Nasty Lately

On Tuesday morning, I checked on the snakes. I was proud of myself because they hadn't made it out of the tanks for a few weeks. I couldn't even remember the last time my sisters or my parents complained about them.

Then I went out in the yard to check on the turkey. He seemed pretty happy to see me. I'd never really spent time with a turkey before. I decided to name him Turkey Sandwich.

Darwin was still in bed, so I went up to check on him. He was awake and watching TV.

"How do you feel?" I asked.

"Like I was stung by every mosquito from here to Florida. My body itches so bad, it's humming."

"That stinks. Hey, I named our new friend out there Turkey Sandwich. What do you think?"

"That's awesome! Turkey Sandwich," he repeated and laughed.

"Why do you have my socks on your hands?"

"Your mom gave them to me to keep me from scratching. Thanks for letting me stay in your bed. I don't think I could have slept on the floor in the sleeping bag last night."

"No problem." I felt really bad for Darwin. I guessed having him sleep in my bed wasn't such a big deal compared to how uncomfortable he felt. "Hey, we're having a Thanksgiving feast at my school today. My teacher's having parents make the food the way they did in the olden days, and we're going to eat with our hands and stuff. It'll probably be lame, but if you feel up to it, you should come up. It's at one o'clock. You could walk up there if you want. The school's two blocks up the road, or I'm sure my mom or dad would drive you."

"Thanks, Justin. You're my favorite boy cousin," he said.

"Thanks, but I'm your only boy cousin," I reminded him.

"True, but you're still the best one."

"Thanks. You're pretty cool too. Maybe I'll see you later."

I walked to school because the weather was really nice. Mom and Dad said they'd be up for the feast at one. I was so excited to get through the day and have a five-day break for Thanksgiving.

I had to admit that Mrs. Cliff was pretty nice over the days leading up to Thanksgiving. I unpacked and sat down at my desk.

"Justin, I've noticed you've been much more behaved these past few days. I wanted you to know I'm proud of you for that."

"Thanks, Mrs. Cliff. I was just thinking how you haven't been that nasty the past few days. I mean to say, you've been really nice lately too. Thanks. I don't want to get in trouble, so I should probably stop talking."

"That might be a good idea," she said.

16
Eat Up

We had to have the feast inside because it started raining really hard around eleven. We worked together all morning getting the last-minute decorations up on the walls, putting on our costumes, and setting the class for the feast. Half the kids in the class were Pilgrims, and the others were Native Americans. I was a Pilgrim with a tall black hat and a collared shirt. It was actually kind of fun.

The room looked pretty good by the time the parents arrived. They sat where they could, and the kids stood because Mrs. Cliff reminded us that at the first Thanksgiving, the children didn't sit. I actually liked standing more because I don't like sitting all day long at school.

Mrs. Cliff explained that at the first Thanksgiving they probably didn't have dessert after the meal, so we could choose to have dessert first if we wanted. The kids all cheered. But as the parents put out the food, it became clear that their Thanksgiving desserts weren't what we were expecting. There were no pies, and everything that was supposed to be a dessert tasted pretty gross.

"If you remember, there wasn't any sugar, so the desserts weren't sweet like we're used to today," Mrs. Cliff reminded us.

May said, "If I'd lived back then, I don't think I would have eaten a whole lot of dessert."

"I understand," Mrs. Cliff said. "Also, they would have had a lot of meat. Historical records indicate that the main meat at the feast was venison. Does anyone know what that is?"

Cameron raised his hand. "It's deer meat."

"You're right. They would have eaten deer meat and some wild birds for sure. No one can say for certain if they had turkey or not."

Cameron's dad walked around the table and offered everyone a plate of venison. Most of the kids didn't try it. Dad and I did, and it tasted pretty good. The best part was we had to eat it with our hands.

"We should do this at home," I said to Mom.

"For someone who complains about school all the time, you seem to be having a pretty good time, Mr. Pilgrim."

"It's not usually like this," I said. "It's usually much more boring and lame. Today is pretty cool, though."

The rain outside was really picking up. The parking lot was starting to fill with puddles. The adults all said stuff like, "It's a good thing we didn't have the feast outside." Mrs. Cliff seemed to be having a great time all dressed up as a Native American woman.

Mrs. Cliff stood up and spoke to the group again. "We'll have turkey today, but on the real Thanksgiving, they may have had swan or other wild birds too. Since we don't eat swan, we'll go with turkeys."

Two of the parents brought in cooked turkeys and placed them on the table. I couldn't help but think of my poor buddy Turkey Sandwich at home in the rain. I helped pass the turkey plate along to the next person and thought, *You're a lucky bird, Turkey Sandwich.*

Then Mrs. Cliff explained that the first Thanksgiving probably had a lot of seafood. The parents brought in a few lobsters, a few cooked fish, and some clams. She explained that the first Thanksgiving might have included seal meat, but we certainly were not going to eat that.

The amount of food on the table was amazing. It was also kind of gross because everyone was eating with their hands and wiping them on the tablecloth. Mrs. Cliff told us that it was all right because that was the way they did it at the first Thanksgiving. They didn't worry too much about manners or being neat when they ate.

I couldn't help imagining what it would be like if the whole thing broke out into the greatest food fight in the history of the world. I imagined what I would do first if it started. I decided I would throw a lobster at Cameron for getting me in trouble around Halloween. He'd probably retaliate with the whole fish that was resting in front of him. From there the entire room would explode into a wild food disaster. It would be awesome.

I was snapped out of my fantasy by May. "Who's that?" she said, pointing to the window.

Someone was standing at the window looking in. He was soaking wet and carrying a crate by a handle. Lightning cracked, and the flash made the person at the window look like something out of a monster movie.

17
The True Meaning

Mrs. Cliff went to the window. "You have to go around to the front if you are trying to get in the school," she called over the sound of the rain.

I heard the person at the window say, "I'm Justin's cousin Darwin. He said I could come to the feast."

The noise from the feast was so loud that it was hard to hear. "Mom, I think that's Darwin," I said.

"Mrs. Cliff," I said, "it's my cousin Darwin. He's visiting from Florida."

Mrs. Cliff opened the door and let him in. He set his crate, which was covered by a blanket, on the floor. He was soaking wet and looked like he'd just taken a ride down a flume. I went to the closet and got him my coat to warm up.

"Hey, why'd you walk here in this crazy rain?" I asked.

"You invited me. I didn't want to be rude."

I noticed a few of the kids whispering and pointing toward Darwin. He noticed it too.

"Is it all right that I'm here?" he asked.

"Of course it is," Mrs. Cliff said. "The more the merrier." I could see that Mrs. Cliff had gotten a whiff of his breath because she made a face and waved a bit at the air. She also smiled uncomfortably when she saw his massive case of poison ivy.

May waved me over. I walked over to her and leaned in. "What?" I asked.

"What's wrong with his face? He looks like a monster or something."

"He has poison ivy. It's fine."

"I don't want to get poison ivy," Karen said, overhearing me.

I walked to the front of the room and stood with Darwin. "Everyone," I announced, "this is my cousin Darwin. He's covered from head to toe with the worst poison ivy I've ever seen, but he walked all the way up here to come to our feast. I hope you'll make him feel welcome."

Mrs. Cliff clapped her hands and looked as though she might cry. "Justin, I didn't think you were learning anything in my class this year," she said.

"I'm not," I said.

"Very funny. But I see that by inviting your cousin to join our feast, you opened yourself to the true meaning of Thanksgiving. It's about sharing and welcoming new people who might be very different from you."

That's when a turkey sound came from the crate on the floor. "I brought Turkey Sandwich," Darwin said. "Is that cool?"

"You brought a turkey sandwich?" Mrs. Cliff asked.

"No," I said. "He brought a real turkey. Its name is Turkey Sandwich."

"Justin said you guys were celebrating an old-time Thanksgiving. Back then, guests would have brought a turkey. So I brought a turkey. Plus, it was raining like crazy, and I felt bad for the little guy."

Mrs. Cliff peeked under the blanket and looked like she'd seen a ghost. "Well, I see you did. You shouldn't have. You really shouldn't have. But I guess it's all right if we leave him in the crate. The kids can take turns taking a look at a turkey before it's cooked."

I could tell Mrs. Cliff was struggling to make a connection to learning so the turkey could stay. She told the class they could take a look at Turkey Sandwich as long as they kept their hands out of the crate. She made me promise not to let him out under any circumstance. I promised.

"I haven't eaten since yesterday," Darwin interrupted. "Does the true meaning of Thanksgiving also include me eating something?"

"Of course, please sit down and help yourself," Mrs. Cliff insisted.

18
A Thanksgiving Miracle

The feast was awesome. Mrs. Cliff even invited Mrs. Fiesta's class to join us. They were in costumes too, and the whole scene was pretty amazing. Darwin was so hungry that he kept eating and eating. I couldn't believe how much he was putting back, but he hadn't eaten in a whole day because he'd been so uncomfortable the day before.

Mom nudged me. "It was really nice of you to include your cousin," she said.

"Thanks. He's really cool, if you can get past the breath thing. I don't mind if he sleeps in my bed. I'm sorry I was giving you a hard time about that the other day."

"It's all right," Mom said. "Justin, I hope you're starting to realize that one of the biggest reasons you hate school so much is your attitude about it, not Mrs. Cliff. Today, you have a great attitude, and you're having a great day. You should try this every day, and who knows? Maybe school won't be such a nightmare for you."

"You make some interesting points," I said. "But on most days, it's not me. School really is a nightmare."

"Let's agree to disagree. Why don't you do me a favor and get me a piece of the pumpkin pie I brought. It's in a box on your desk. This stuff isn't doing it for me."

"Okay," I said, slowly getting up to go get the pie. As soon as I was out of the seat, I heard everyone react to something. I turned back over my shoulder to see that Darwin had thrown up all over my chair. I mean he exploded! If I hadn't stood up, I would have been covered. Mom was shocked but fine. Somehow Darwin had managed not to barf on anyone. The room fell completely silent, and everyone kind of looked at each other, processing what had happened.

Darwin spoke first. "That was me. That was totally on me. Sorry, everyone. I'm not used to eating so much deer meat."

It was one of the strangest things I'd ever seen, but it was also one of the most magical. It was a miracle that I didn't get hit. It was truly a Thanksgiving miracle.

19
Be Free

By the time the real Thanksgiving rolled around on Thursday, Darwin's poison ivy was much better. For the first time in my life, I was actually excited about Thanksgiving. I kind of understood what Mrs. Cliff was talking about. Thanksgiving is one of those holidays it's hard to really understand until you sit down with a bunch of people you wouldn't normally eat with and you have a good time.

Looking back on the weeks leading up to Halloween and Thanksgiving, I wasn't sure why

I'd gotten in so much trouble. Mom said the reason school was such a problem for me was because of my attitude. I couldn't help thinking about what she said. I didn't think she was right, but I'd keep thinking about it.

The Thanksgiving meal we shared with Darwin and his Mom was great—not $3,000 great, but still great. After dinner, we all went outside to set Turkey Sandwich free.

I carried him to the edge of our property where the fence opens to the woods. "I'd like to say a few words about my good friend Turkey Sandwich."

"Come on," Becky said.

"It's freezing out here," Mindy said.

"Go ahead," Dad said.

"A few weeks ago, I didn't really appreciate Thanksgiving or my cousin Darwin," I began. "I even called him Yuck Mouth behind his back. Sorry, cousin, but your breath is really bad. You have to start brushing your teeth, or they're going to fall out by the time you're in middle school."

"Justin!" Mom said.

"It's all right," Darwin said. "He's right. My dentist told me the same thing. He's just being honest. That's what Thanksgiving is all about."

"No, it's not," Becky said.

"Either way," I said, "a few weeks ago, I didn't appreciate Thanksgiving. I also didn't realize what a fun cousin I had. If it wasn't for this turkey, Turkey Sandwich, we probably wouldn't have had such a great couple of days. And so, on this Thanksgiving, while the rest of America eats turkey by the forkful, we release one back into the wild."

"This is ridiculous," Mindy said.

"No, it's not," Darwin said. "This little turkey is a magical little bird. I think we should release him and then go catch him again tomorrow."

"That's the best idea I've heard all day." We threw open the gate to the backyard. "Be free!" I shouted, but Turkey Sandwich walked back toward the house and away from the woods. I picked him up and carried him out of the yard again. I placed him down at the edge of the woods. We all laughed when he walked back through the fence and into the yard.

"Great," Becky said.

"Now this crazy bird doesn't want to go?" Mindy added.

"Can I keep him?" I asked Mom.

"Leave the gate open, and he'll probably be gone in the morning. I'm going inside. It's freezing," she said. The rest of the family went back inside too.

"Thanks," Darwin said. "This was the best Thanksgiving ever."

"It totally was," I agreed.

Made in the USA
Charleston, SC
07 January 2016

ne heure de marche, elles traversent une voie
Les éclaireurs signalent un convoi à quelques
nord.

quante hommes avec moi ! clame Spartacus.
end à l'endroit indiqué et découvre une caravane
Surpris par la tempête, vingt chariots de ravi-
t sont prisonniers de la glace. À la vue des rebelles,
ts de la petite escorte prennent la fuite. Plus légers,
es les rejoignent. Le combat est bref. En quelques
le sang des légionnaires macule la neige.
tôt, les hommes de Spartacus fouillent sous les

ssus est généreux ! braille Dragma en brandis-
amphore.
acus, lui, se préoccupe des chevaux. Son armée
les siens à Rhegium. Les quarante bêtes de trait
oureuses. Spartacus ordonne à ses soldats de les
Il choisit le sien, un cheval noir au large poitrail.
ous en faudra d'autres, et rapidement, dit-il.
valerie joue un rôle essentiel dans sa stratégie.
voyons une commande à Crassus ! plaisante
, occupé à dévorer un quartier de viande fumée.
acus lui adresse un regard réprobateur :
n'es pas seul à être affamé. Il faut partager !
me le vin ? ricane Dragma entre deux goulées.
acus ne relève pas la plaisanterie. Il pense à Crassus,
gnore la position. Le proconsul peut surgir d'une
l'autre.
route, pressons !
ommes chargent à la hâte les vivres sur les che-

Chapitre 21

La tempête
janvier 71 av. J. C.

La neige a commencé à tomber dès le lever du soleil. Lourde, épaisse, obstinée, elle recouvre la forêt, le fossé et le mur, et adoucit les lignes du champ de guerre.

Vers le soir, un vent violent se lève, apportant une neige dure qui s'accumule sur les fortifications et noie les feux romains. Les guetteurs, aveuglés, ne distinguent plus l'enceinte. Un casque de glace se forme sur leur casque de fer. Leurs bottes glissent sur le sol gelé. Les rafales hurlantes emportent les cris des sentinelles.

— C'est le moment, dit Spartacus.

Toute la journée, des milliers d'hommes, cachés dans la forêt, ont préparé l'assaut. Une première vague transporte des branches et les jette dans le fossé. Elle est suivie d'une deuxième chargée de sacs de terre. Les esclaves la déversent et tassent le sol. La neige épaisse étouffe les bruits. Sur une longueur de deux cents pas, la tranchée est comblée.

Soudain, des lueurs dansent le long du mur. Les rebelles se couchent et restent immobiles. Des Romains passent, munis de torches. Ils s'éloignent, malmenés par la tempête. L'obscurité revient. Au signal, les esclaves se dressent. L'instant est venu.

— Les échelles ! commande Spartacus.

L'ordre se transmet d'une cohorte à l'autre. Trente échelles sortent de la forêt et se dressent contre le mur d'enceinte. De l'autre côté, tout est calme. Sur les tours, les guetteurs luttent contre les rafales. En bas, dans leurs tentes à moitié enfouies sous la neige, les légionnaires se chauffent autour de leurs braseros.

Les esclaves ont endossé des fourrures et enveloppé

leurs armes pour éviter de réveil[...] tains escaladent les tours, d'aut[...] tentes. En quelques minutes, les p[...] tralisés. Les hurlements de la tem[...] victimes. La voie est libre.

Une torche, agitée au somm[...] signal. Les rebelles s'avancent e[...] sent les échelles dans le plus gra[...] regroupent les escouades. Les re[...] serrées jusqu'à l'aube pour mettr[...] sible entre eux et l'armée ennem[...]

Lorsque le jour paraît, ils se re[...] à des milles au nord. La tempê[...] perce les nuages, révélant un p[...] éblouissante. Ils sont trente mill[...] triomphante.

Spartacus circule parmi eux. Il [...] Oppius, Afer, Dragma, Marcus[...] d'enfants et de blessés sont rest[...] dant, les guerriers continuent à[...] rejoignent l'armée par petits grou[...] la montagne à la recherche de le[...]

— Où allons-nous ? demande[...] Spartacus indique les monts [...]

— Là-haut, d'abord, puis nou[...]

Aucun ne songe à contester [...] plus, Spartacus a fait preuve de s[...] tant favorable et sa patience a p[...]

Vers midi, les colonnes prog[...] montagne. Le froid, de plus en [...]

Aprè[...]
roma[...]
mille[...]

Il [...]
roma[...]
taille[...]
les so[...]
les es[...]
minut[...]

Au [...]
bâche[...]

— [...]
sant u[...]

Sp[...]
a laiss[...]
sont v[...]
détele[...]

— [...]
La [...]

— [...]
Kalan[...]
Spa[...]

— [...]
— M[...]
Spa[...]
dont il [...]
heure [...]

— E[...]
Ses [...]

vaux et les tirent dans la neige profonde. À la vue de cette nourriture providentielle, leurs compagnons poussent des hurlements de joie.

— Spartacus, tu es un magicien ! crie Argétorix.

Le chef des esclaves sourit amèrement. La veille, il n'était qu'un maladroit, coupable d'avoir conduit ses hommes dans un piège mortel.

Il a baptisé son cheval Niger. Il le conduit par la bride après avoir hissé Delia sur son dos. Kalanos marche à leur côté. Il montre le soleil à la jeune femme :

— Regarde comme il brille. C'est celui que tu as vu en rêve : le soleil de la victoire.

— Un soleil indésirable, regrette Spartacus. La tempête aurait effacé nos traces ; le soleil les révèle. Crassus saura où nous trouver.

— Qu'il nous trouve ! rugit Dragma. Plus de mur entre nous. Il est vulnérable et nous sommes invincibles !

« Le vin lui monte à la tête ! » songe Spartacus.

— Nous serons invincibles tant que nous resterons unis !

Les hommes approuvent. Spartacus les regarde rire et chanter tandis qu'ils abordent le chemin de la montagne. Derrière leur euphorie, il distingue leurs dissensions. Dragma voudrait prendre la route du nord. Kalanos parle de survivre dans les monts du Bruttium. Afer envisage de se diriger vers Petelia, à l'ouest. Entre ces divergences, Spartacus a du mal à imposer ses vues. L'épreuve de Rhegium, les privations, les échecs ont affaibli son autorité. Il est maintenant forcé d'imposer sa loi par la violence.

— Explique-leur ce que tu veux faire, conseille Delia.

Il regarde sa compagne d'un air désabusé :

— Si au moins je le savais ! Ma décision dépend de celle de Crassus. Quand j'aurai découvert ses projets, je bâtirai un plan. Dans l'immédiat, je suis dans le brouillard. Dès qu'il découvrira notre percée, il remontera vers la Campanie pour barrer les routes de Rome, je suppose. Pas question d'aller par là. L'armée est affaiblie. Nous devons organiser le ravitaillement, trouver un refuge, pratiquer la guérilla. Dans quelques semaines, nous irons vers l'est. Nous remonterons le long du littoral de la mer Adriatique. Qu'en penses-tu ?

La jeune Ibère, bercée par le balancement du cheval, a fermé les yeux. On dirait qu'elle n'a pas entendu la question. Puis elle soupire :

— Je ne vois plus rien, tu le sais.

La voix est lasse. Spartacus se demande si Delia a perdu son don de divination ou si elle refuse de lui dévoiler un destin tragique.

Chapitre 22

La montagne rouge
février 71 av. J. C.

Marcus Licinius Crassus ne décolère pas. Les esclaves condamnés à se rendre ou à mourir ont réussi à s'évader dans des conditions inadmissibles. La tempête les a aidés, c'est certain, mais l'incompétence des officiers romains est la vraie responsable de cet échec. Au lieu de renforcer la surveillance, ils se sont laissé endormir.

L'armée rebelle a défilé sous leurs yeux sans rencontrer d'opposition. Cinquante mille hommes ! C'est à peine croyable.

La fureur du proconsul vise ses tribuns. Elle s'adresse aussi à lui-même, à son manque de sang-froid. Redoutant que Spartacus, ce diable d'homme intelligent et audacieux, ne fonce sur Rome, il a demandé au Sénat d'ordonner le retour de Pompée et de ses légions d'Ibérie.

Il a commis ainsi la pire des erreurs. Pompée, son rival, n'aura qu'à se montrer pour récolter les fruits d'une victoire à laquelle il est étranger. Car c'est lui, Crassus, qui a pris tous les risques, affronté tous les dangers.

À présent, il est trop tard pour revenir en arrière. Pompée ne s'est pas fait prier pour répondre à l'appel du Sénat. Il sera bientôt là. Il ne reste plus à Crassus qu'à triompher avant l'arrivée du vainqueur de Sertorius.

Conscients de la colère du proconsul, les tribuns attendent ses ordres dans le plus profond silence.

— Combien reste-t-il d'esclaves ? finit par dire Crassus.

Clodius fait un pas en avant :

— Quinze mille, général.

— Tu es sûr de tes renseignements ?

— Les transfuges semblent sincères.

— Des esclaves sincères ! grogne Crassus méprisant.

— Ils espèrent notre clémence.

— Ou nous attirer dans un piège, un de plus !

— Nos éclaireurs corroborent leurs affirmations. Deux lieutenants de Spartacus, Gannicus et Castus, commandent les rebelles.

Le proconsul médite en silence, puis il se décide :

— Je pense que les déserteurs disent la vérité. Cependant, on n'est jamais assez prudent : qu'on les torture !

Le supplice confirme les attestations des esclaves repentis : une bande de Gaulois et de Germains s'avance imprudemment jusqu'au pied du mont Bellinum. Par une manœuvre habile, Crassus les encercle. Sa troupe est trois fois plus importante que celle de ses adversaires.

— Pas de prisonniers ! ordonne-t-il.

Au son des trompettes, ses huit légions s'avancent, précédées de six cohortes d'auxiliaires. Pour se défendre, Gannicus et Castus ont disposé leurs hommes en cercle. À un signal, ils prennent follement l'offensive. Et le massacre commence. Avec leur équipement léger, les rebelles sont une proie facile pour les légionnaires solidement cuirassés.

Crassus se réjouit. En divisant ses forces, Spartacus se livre à sa merci. Deux semaines auparavant, le proconsul a déjà exterminé dix mille esclaves au bord du golfe de Tarente. « Spartacus, je t'ai surestimé ! » Il a parlé trop fort et trop vite : le champ de bataille est couvert de morts et Crassus calcule le temps qui reste avant la destruction totale de l'armée rebelle lorsque des sonneries retentissent de tous côtés.

Les trompettes sont romaines, mais ceux qui les utilisent sont des esclaves. Ils surgissent sur les sommets environnants. C'est un spectacle terrifiant de les voir dévaler les pentes en rangs serrés comme la lave d'un volcan.

Les Romains résistent au choc de la horde au prix de lourdes pertes. Harcelés de flèches, de javelots et de pierres, ils tombent. Des esclaves au comble de la folie se jettent dans la mêlée. Le corps à corps féroce tourne à l'avantage des rebelles. Les légions cèdent. Sur le flanc de la montagne, où se déroulent les combats les plus sanglants, des cris s'élèvent, un chant guerrier :

— Spartacus !

— Spartacus !

— Spartacus !

Toute l'armée rebelle est là. La rage au cœur, Crassus doit se résoudre à ordonner la retraite. Les esclaves qu'on croyait vaincus restent maîtres du champ de bataille. Cependant, ils ont payé un lourd tribut : vingt mille hommes gisent sur le sol. La terre est inondée de sang.

— La montagne est rouge, la couleur des dieux ! crie Dragma, ivre de carnage. Tu as vaincu, une fois encore, Spartacus.

Le chef des révoltés contemple en silence le champ couvert de morts. Il a repoussé l'ennemi. Cependant, après chaque victoire, ses forces s'amenuisent. « Jusqu'à quand allons-nous résister ? » se demande-t-il.

Delia détourne la tête quand ses yeux l'interrogent. Spartacus la soupçonne d'avoir la réponse à cette question. L'Ibère fait semblant de l'ignorer.

Ses soldats l'adulent comme autrefois, depuis qu'il a

renoué avec la victoire. Ils se croient invincibles. Marcus est l'un des rares à comprendre que son succès est dû à la chance. L'armée n'aurait pas dû se trouver sur le mont Bellinum, mais plus à l'est. Gannicus et Castus ont désobéi à ses ordres et l'ont payé de leur vie. Les vainqueurs se persuadent que leur imprudence faisait partie d'une stratégie. Ils ont servi d'appât pour surprendre l'ennemi.

En un sens, ils ont raison. Les succès de Spartacus sont souvent imprévisibles. Alors que la tactique des Romains est toujours la même, la sienne naît des circonstances. Ses adversaires sont incapables de prévoir ses réactions. Il les ignore lui-même. Il n'a qu'une certitude : il luttera jusqu'à la mort.

— Et maintenant ? Où allons-nous ? demande Marcus à voix basse.

Spartacus regarde le jeune homme avec amitié. Pour la première fois, le précepteur s'est battu comme ses compagnons. Si l'épée suspendue à son baudrier paraît trop lourde pour lui, il arbore avec fierté une blessure au visage, une estafilade peu profonde, d'où s'écoule un sang qu'il se garde bien d'étancher.

Spartacus montre le sommet du Bellinum :

— Nous allons camper là-haut. Puis nous irons à Brindes. Nous nous emparerons des bateaux de la flotte marchande.

— Et ensuite ?

— La Sicile ou la Sardaigne.

— Il nous faudra beaucoup de navires !

Spartacus hausse les épaules :

— Qui sait combien nous serons, une fois arrivés au port ?

Chapitre 23

Contre-attaque
février 71 av. J. C.

Du sommet de l'arbre, le guetteur agite un fanion.

— Les voici ! dit Dragma.

Quelques minutes plus tard, les rebelles, embusqués dans la forêt, aperçoivent les cinq cents cavaliers de Lucius Quinctius. Le préfet a commis l'erreur de se séparer de l'infanterie romaine. La légion, commandée par le questeur Cneius Scrofa, est moins vulnérable que ses cavaliers dans cette zone accidentée. Les bandes de traînards qu'il a repérées et massacrées sur son chemin ont convaincu le maître de la cavalerie que l'armée rebelle était aux abois.

Spartacus l'a laissé triompher et s'avancer jusqu'au cœur de la montagne. Il a imaginé lui-même le piège vers lequel il attire le présomptueux. Le plus difficile est de retenir ses hommes massés sur les pentes et altérés de sang romain.

Il va d'un groupe à l'autre, rappelant ses consignes :

— N'attaquez pas avant le signal. Tuez les cavaliers, épargnez les chevaux. Cachez les torches.

Ses lieutenants calment l'impatience de leurs soldats.

— Attendez ! Attendez encore !

La distance augmente encore entre la cavalerie et l'infanterie romaines. Les cavaliers de Quinctius sont à portée de tir.

— Préparez-vous ! lance Spartacus.

Il lève la main. Une trompette sonne par trois fois. Une barrière de flammes jaillit soudain devant l'escadron romain lancé au galop. Les chevaux se cabrent, désarçonnant les cavaliers. Une nuée de flèches, jaillie des arbres, surprend les Romains. Le préfet commande à ses hommes de se replier. L'ordre est aussitôt exécuté. Les cavaliers font volte-face et repartent à bride abattue lorsqu'une deuxième barrière de flammes leur coupe la retraite. Le piège s'est refermé sur eux.

Un certain nombre de cavaliers parvient à franchir les flammes et à se sauver. La majorité succombe ou se rend.

Le combat a alerté l'infanterie romaine qui se trouve à deux milles en arrière. Scrofa s'élance au secours de la cavalerie avec un corps d'auxiliaires et une demi-légion. Il a tout juste le temps de ranger sa troupe en ordre de bataille avant d'être assailli de tous côtés.

Les flèches et les javelots s'abattent sur les légionnaires en position de tortue. Les esclaves mettent en batterie une catapulte prise au cours de la bataille du mont Bellinum. Les quartiers de roc emportent les boucliers et fauchent les Romains.

Une flèche blesse le questeur à la cuisse droite. Deux de ses officiers sont tués. Les légionnaires abritent leur chef sous leurs boucliers. Ils se replient ainsi au prix de lourdes pertes.

— Poursuivez-les ! ordonne Spartacus.

Les vélites sortent de la forêt. Puis un corps de rebelles lourdement armés se précipite sur les Romains.

— Restez en position ! crie Scrofa.

Pendant quelques minutes, les légionnaires font face à leurs adversaires avec courage. Mais la débandade des cavaliers finit par entraîner celle des fantassins. L'armée romaine se replie en désordre vers la vallée de Venusinus, où campent les légions de Crassus.

Spartacus donne l'ordre d'interrompre la poursuite avant la fin du jour. Ses hommes obéissent avec réticence.

— Pourquoi ne pas massacrer ces chiens jusqu'au dernier ? s'insurge Dragma.

— Pour éviter de commettre la même erreur qu'eux. Ils nous attireraient dans la plaine où nous serions à la merci de Crassus.

— Tu es devenu bien prudent ! constate Kalanos avec une ironie blessante.

Spartacus plonge ses yeux au fond des siens :

— Lâche ?

— Tu es le plus courageux d'entre nous !

En disant cela, Afer repousse Kalanos et regarde ses compagnons d'un air menaçant comme pour les mettre au défi de prétendre le contraire.

Le soir, dans son abri des monts Alba, l'état-major de Spartacus discute âprement. Argétorix parle de rester dans ce refuge inaccessible :

— Dans la montagne, nous avons une chance de survivre. Pour nous atteindre, les Romains seront obligés de diviser leurs forces. Dans la plaine, c'est l'inverse.

— Il faut attaquer ! Une victoire contre Crassus nous ouvrirait la route du nord, s'entête Kalanos.

Dragma l'approuve :

— Avec les compagnons qui nous ont rejoints, nous sommes cinquante mille. Assez pour vaincre les Romains. Beaucoup trop pour subsister dans ce pays désert.

— Le ravitaillement est difficile, admet Marcus. Nos caravanes sont interceptées, nos escortes massacrées.

— Elles circulent mieux la nuit.

— Les sources d'approvisionnement sont de plus en

plus lointaines, dit Marcus. Les Romains surveillent les routes.

Spartacus lève la main pour demander la parole :

— Pas question d'exposer des centaines d'hommes pour en nourrir des milliers. J'ai besoin de l'armée tout entière pour gagner Brindes et quitter l'Italie.

— Nos hommes sont las de fuir, proteste Dragma.

— Qui parle de fuir ? gronde Spartacus. La marche vers l'Adriatique n'est pas un exode, c'est une offensive.

— Crassus se lancera à ta poursuite, fait remarquer Kalanos. Pour un guerrier qui ne veut pas avoir son ennemi derrière lui, tu vas être servi !

— Dans ce cas, il sera temps de l'affronter. Comme nous l'avons fait aujourd'hui. Cette victoire est précieuse : nous avons pris trois cents chevaux.

— Et deux cents prisonniers, ajoute Afer. Que faisons-nous d'eux ?

— Libère-les !

Ils regardent leur chef avec stupeur. Puis ils se mettent à parler tous à la fois :

— Tu veux les épargner ?

— Ils reprendront aussitôt les armes !

— Pour nous massacrer !

— Tu te figures que Crassus se montrera miséricor-dieux parce que tu as fait grâce à ses soldats ?

Spartacus se passe la main sur les yeux :

— Je n'attends rien des Romains, sauf de la cruauté. Mais je suis fatigué de massacrer des hommes sans défense.

— Organisons des combats de gladiateurs ! s'écrie Afer.

— Assez de ces jeux funèbres ! soupire Spartacus. Depuis

deux ans, nous sommes devenus des hommes libres. Nous avons donné à nos ennemis des leçons de courage. Le temps est venu de leur donner une leçon d'humanité.

— Crassus a besoin des deux ! s'esclaffe Dragma.

Marcus fait la moue :

— Je doute qu'il soit bon élève dans ces matières !

Les hommes se tordent de rire.

Deux vieilles femmes s'approchent des feux. Elles apportent à manger aux officiers. Delia et Phryné viennent à leur tour, bavardes et souriantes. Depuis longtemps Spartacus n'a pas vu un soupçon de gaieté sur le visage de la jeune Ibère. Il résiste à l'envie de lui en demander la cause par crainte de dissiper cette expression qui la rajeunit.

Delia et Phryné ont combattu comme les hommes. Pourtant, elles ne semblent pas le moins du monde fatiguées, contrairement aux officiers qui s'assoupissent devant le feu, leur ragoût avalé.

— La nuit est belle ! murmure Spartacus en s'étirant.

L'odeur des arbres lui rappelle les senteurs des forêts thraces de son enfance. Ces souvenirs lui semblent appartenir à une autre vie.

Chapitre 24

Mourir avec honneur
mars 71 av. J. C.

« Tu t'es enfin décidé ! » Les regards disent tous la même chose, mais avec des intentions différentes. Dragma exprime l'admiration, Afer l'impatience, Marcus la peur, Delia l'indifférence, ou le fatalisme, comme si elle connaissait déjà la suite de l'aventure.

— Pourquoi avoir renoncé à Brindes ? demande Marcus avec une nuance de reproche.

Spartacus répond d'une voix sourde, les yeux fixés au loin :

— Pour une raison impérieuse : Metellus vient de débarquer là-bas avec ses légions d'Asie.

— Metellus, le consul ?

— Non, son frère, Terentius. Après la défaite de Mithridate, il fallait s'y attendre. Et ce n'est pas tout : Pompée est en Gaule cisalpine. Il arrive par le nord. Nous risquons d'être pris au piège entre leurs deux armées.

— C'est pour ça qu'il faut se débarrasser en vitesse de Crassus, explique Dragma d'un air joyeux.

« Se dépêcher de mourir ! » songe Marcus avec angoisse. Il savait depuis toujours que leur histoire se terminerait ainsi. Mais si tôt…

— Pourquoi ne pas nous réfugier sur les nids d'aigle du Bruttium ? dit-il. Les Romains auraient du mal à nous déloger. Tu l'as répété bien des fois : la guérilla est le seul moyen de les vaincre.

— À condition de rester unis, soupire Spartacus. Ce n'est plus le cas. Les hommes sont impatients de livrer bataille. Si je ne les mène pas au combat, ils iront sans moi.

— Tu as des milliers de fidèles, ceux-là t'obéiront. Tu n'as qu'un mot à dire…

Le visage de Spartacus, marqué par les veilles et les privations, s'illumine. Sa voix tremble. Pendant un bref instant, il retrouve sa jeunesse.

— Je crois qu'ils ont raison : mieux vaut mourir en beauté. Ce sera un combat magnifique.

Oppius, qui affûte son épée sur une pierre dure, relève la tête et grimace un sourire :

— Un combat dont on parlera longtemps.

— Mais toi tu ne seras plus là pour l'entendre ! dit Marcus.

Kalanos se frappe le front comme touché par l'inspiration :

— Il faudrait attirer Crassus dans la vallée de Suburana, utiliser la technique de Spoletium. Tu te souviens ? Tu as cloué les deux consuls au centre pendant qu'on contournait leurs lignes.

Il trace un demi-cercle sur le sol avec la pointe de son glaive avant de poursuivre :

— Ensuite, avec la cavalerie…

— Il n'est plus temps de rêver ! l'interrompt sèchement Spartacus. Crassus est pressé d'en finir, certes, mais pas au point de commettre une imprudence. Il sacrifiera quelques cohortes, des auxiliaires. Ensuite, lorsque nous les aurons détruites, il lancera son infanterie sur nos positions. Nos deux armées sont à peu près de forces égales : cinquante mille hommes. Leurs soldats sont plus aguerris ; les nôtres plus déterminés.

Il regarde le ciel. Le temps est beau, sans un souffle de vent. Dans la plaine, l'herbe est sèche comme en plein été. Les étendards qu'il a conquis pendent le long de leurs mâts.

Les deux camps, celui de Crassus et celui des rebelles, se dressent à six milles de distance. Ils se ressemblent : même fossé, même *agger**, même palissade, même écran massif protégeant les quatre portes reliées par des allées en croix. Spartacus utilise les techniques romaines en les adaptant à ses contraintes.

Pour la bataille qui se prépare, il a imaginé une tactique inspirée de celle de ses adversaires. Cependant, ses troupes manquent de discipline, et ceux qui incarnaient l'autorité sont morts. Les officiers qui les remplacent ont du mal à se faire obéir.

La nuit est paisible. Les jours qui suivent le sont aussi. Sur le champ de bataille qui n'est encore qu'une pâture, le temps paraît suspendu. La destinée retient son souffle. Un rapace solitaire plane en cercle avec un cri sauvage, invitation à la cruauté.

De temps en temps, un petit groupe de cavaliers romains vient galoper autour du camp des esclaves pour s'assurer, sans doute, que l'adversaire est toujours là. Ces éclaireurs restent prudemment hors de portée des archers. Après un tour, ils repartent et disparaissent.

— Demain, dit Spartacus.

Dragma émet un grognement approbateur :

— Les hommes s'agitent à la manière des fauves qui ont flairé l'odeur du sang.

— Ne les nourris pas trop. Qu'ils gardent de l'appétit pour le festin que je vais leur offrir !

Cette bravade réjouit les chefs. Les premiers à s'être révoltés retrouvent le Spartacus du début, celui qui prenait toujours l'initiative du combat et les menait à la victoire.

Ils sont près de cent, assis en lignes superposées sur la pente qui monte vers le fossé. La lueur des feux donne à leurs visages un air cruel.

Seul, debout devant eux, Spartacus explique une dernière fois sa stratégie : détruire les vélites avant d'attaquer l'infanterie lourde. Renforcer les ailes pour éviter de se laisser envelopper par la cavalerie…

— Daria, tu placeras tes archers derrière les écrans. Œnomaüs, avec tes hommes, tu attaqueras l'aile gauche…

Le silence des officiers le rappelle à la réalité. Œnomaüs est mort en Apulie. L'un des lieutenants de Spartacus lève le bras.

— Oppius, oui, c'est toi qui conduiras l'attaque.

L'évocation involontaire du mort est un mauvais présage. Pour conjurer le sort et détendre l'atmosphère, il grommelle :

— Avec votre manie de porter des noms romains…

Ils se mettent tous à rire un peu trop fort. Kalanos lance :

— Et ton nom à toi, où l'as-tu pris ?

— C'est celui d'un guerrier spartiate.

Il a dit ça au hasard. Ils le prennent au sérieux et se taisent.

Machinalement, il frotte son épaule droite marquée d'une vieille blessure. Phénomène étrange, celle-ci devient douloureuse avant chaque combat. Des cicatrices, les hommes qui l'écoutent en sont couverts. Leurs corps racontent en images tous les combats qu'ils ont livrés.

Spartacus lève les yeux sur la voûte constellée d'étoiles :

— Demain sera une belle journée !

Ils l'approuvent avec enthousiasme. La guerre donne

un sens à leur vie, et la mort ne peut être que le prolongement de leur liberté.

À l'aube, les sonneries des trompettes et le branle-bas de combat ont alerté Crassus : l'affrontement est imminent. Il dispose son armée en ordre de bataille. Le dispositif est classique : les vélites devant, la cavalerie aux deux ailes, les légions au centre, entourées par les auxiliaires. Le tout forme un bloc compact, puissant, impressionnant.

Crassus est reconnaissable à son cheval blanc, à son armure aux parements d'or et à son cimier rouge.

« Arriver jusqu'à lui ! s'enflamme Spartacus. Le combattre, le terrasser ! » Sa fièvre est telle que ses mains se mettent à trembler. Pour l'apaiser il empoigne ses deux épées.

Il a chassé son cheval. Cette fois, il combattra à pied, à la tête de ses **fantassins**. À sa droite, il a Delia ; à sa gauche, l'immen**se Zarax, armé** de la masse hérissée de fer, qui a massacré **plus d'enne**mis à lui seul que tous les autres officiers réunis.

Les vélites romains, armés de javelots, s'avancent les premiers. Lorsqu'il les juge à portée de tir, Spartacus donne le signal. Une trompette retentit. Cent archers se dressent et criblent de traits l'infanterie légère qui se replie dans le plus grand désordre. C'est ce que Spartacus a prévu. Il brandit ses deux épées en croix. Aussitôt, les buccins sonnent la charge. L'immense armée rebelle s'ébranle en poussant des hurlements féroces.

Les esclaves couvrent la plaine sur une largeur de trois mille pas, toutes cohortes confondues, et se jettent sur l'infanterie ennemie. Le choc enfonce les premiers rangs des *hastati*. Il ébranle les *principes*. Seuls les vétérans des *hastati* résistent. Le corps à corps est furieux. Une sorte de danse macabre ponctuée de hurlements et de cris d'agonie.

Pendant près d'une heure, les forces s'équilibrent. Puis les Romains prennent l'avantage, irrésistiblement. La cavalerie de Spartacus, inférieure en nombre, a succombé. Les escadrons romains harcèlent les flancs de son armée, y creusent des brèches où s'engouffrent les auxiliaires.

Au centre, les légionnaires poursuivent leur offensive. Les rebelles sont submergés. Cependant, ils continuent à lutter jusqu'à la mort.

Spartacus a terrassé quatre adversaires lorsqu'il chancelle : la pointe d'une lance lui a traversé la cuisse. Il pare un coup de glaive, se courbe pour éviter un javelot. À cet instant, une lame invisible l'atteint à la nuque et le projette à genoux. Ses yeux qui se voilent cherchent Zarax. Il a ordonné au géant de faire en sorte qu'on ne puisse pas le reconnaître : il ne veut pas servir de trophée à Crassus.

Zarax perçoit sa prière. Sa masse s'écrase sur le visage de l'agonisant. Spartacus devient un mort anonyme comme la plupart des quarante mille esclaves qui jonchent le champ de bataille.

Le soir de sa victoire, Crassus remarque, une fois encore, que pas un seul de ses ennemis n'a tourné le dos à l'armée romaine. Un soleil de sang inonde la plaine.

— Combien de prisonniers ? demande le proconsul.

Un tribun tourne la tête vers l'enclos où les esclaves survivants sont parqués comme des bêtes.

— Quelques centaines.

— Il m'en faut cinq ou six mille.

— D'autres bandes ont été signalées.

— Envoie la cavalerie.

— Cette nuit ?

— Demain suffira. Réunis les soldats, je veux m'adresser à eux. C'est une grande victoire !

— Une victoire qui a sauvé Rome, dit le tribun avec enthousiasme. Tu auras droit au triomphe.

Crassus lui retourne un sourire sans joie :

— J'en doute. Rome est trop orgueilleuse pour célébrer une victoire associée à tant de défaites humiliantes.

Chapitre 25

Six mille croix
avril 71 av. J. C.

Crassus n'a pas eu droit au triomphe. Du bout des lèvres, les sénateurs lui ont octroyé l'ovation : le général, couronné de myrte, aura la permission de gravir le chemin du Capitole, sous les acclamations de la foule, pour offrir un sacrifice aux dieux. Maigre récompense !

Cette mesquinerie n'offense pas le proconsul, il s'y attendait. Ce qu'il ne supporte pas, c'est que le triomphe qu'ils lui ont refusé, les sénateurs l'accordent maintenant à son rival. Pompée, élevé au rang des dieux, dressé sur un char et couronné de laurier, défilera majestueusement du Champ de Mars au Capitole, précédé des dignitaires romains et suivi par ses légions en grand uniforme.

« Que les Érinyes les emportent tous ! » fulmine Crassus. Puis un rire silencieux le secoue. Si les hyènes du Sénat croient faire oublier sa victoire, ils se trompent. Son triomphe est sans doute moins glorieux que celui de Pompée, mais il est beaucoup plus grandiose. Pour frapper les esprits, il a imaginé un spectacle horrifiant : de Capoue à Rome, sur près de deux cents kilomètres, le long de la voie Appia, il a ordonné de crucifier six mille esclaves. Soit deux croix face à face tous les soixante mètres.

Les crucifixions ont commencé depuis trois jours et, déjà, le succès est immense. On vient de l'Italie entière pour y assister. Crassus ne se presse pas de rentrer à Rome. Il chemine par petites étapes, précédant le troupeau misérable des condamnés.

Il aurait voulu exhiber les chefs de la révolte, Spartacus, Crixus, Œnomaüs, Dragma, Afer, Kalanos et les autres. Hélas, ils sont tous morts au combat à la tête de leurs guerriers. Pour compléter sa mise en scène macabre, il a dû se saisir des errants, des bandits, des infirmes et même des femmes. Après tout, elles ont combattu comme les hommes. On leur a rasé la tête pour les confondre avec les autres.

Le rythme sonore des marteaux berce les haltes du proconsul. Ses légionnaires travaillent de l'aube au crépuscule. Pour eux, habitués à édifier des palissades, des fortins et des tours, la confection des croix est un travail de charpente comme les autres.

Le montage du *stipes*, la partie verticale, et du *patibulum*, la partie horizontale, s'opère sur le lieu du supplice. Le plus difficile a été de se procurer le bois. On a réquisitionné les poutres dans les villes voisines et abattu des forêts pour les transformer en forêts de croix.

La croix une fois assemblée, on utilise trois clous, deux pour les poignets et un seul pour les pieds, superposés. Le bruit des marteaux couvre les hurlements des suppliciés. Ensuite, on hisse la croix avec des cordes et on introduit sa base dans un trou, puis on la bloque verticalement au moyen de cales de bois.

Le travail est rapide ; la mort lente. Les esclaves mettent parfois trois jours avant de rendre l'âme.

À Capoue, au départ de cette procession funèbre, les corps pourrissent déjà sur leurs croix. Des nuées de corbeaux et de vautours se disputent les proies.

La scène horrible et fascinante attire les foules. Les curieux viennent en famille de Capoue, de Cumes, de Pompéi, de Neapolis, de Bénévent et de vingt autres villes. Les plus nombreux arrivent de Rome. Les patriciens se déplacent à cheval ou en litière. Crassus les reçoit avec faste sous sa tente. Pour l'occasion, il a fait venir les meilleurs vins de Sicile, de Grèce et d'Ibérie.

Après avoir loué sa victoire, les nobles romains vont voir clouer quelques misérables. Les derniers rebelles disparaissent l'un après l'autre. Cependant, avant de mourir, le visage tourné vers le ciel, ils lancent un dernier cri :

– Spartacus !

Un sénateur se tourne avec curiosité vers le proconsul :

– Qui est ce Spartacus ?

Crassus aimerait répondre simplement : « un gladiateur », ou bien : « le chef des rebelles ». Cependant, en rabaissant son adversaire, il minimiserait sa victoire. Aussi, il dit la vérité :

– Spartacus est l'un des ennemis les plus dangereux que Rome ait affrontés.

Table des matières

Lexique

Ad gladios ! : Aux armes !

Agger : Remblai tenant lieu de fortification dans les camps des légions romaines.

Aigle : Emblème des légions romaines.

Auxiliaire : Soldat appartenant à l'infanterie légère étrangère et servant de renforts aux légions romaines.

Baliste : Machine de guerre permettant de lancer des projectiles (pierres, javelots, flèches, etc.).

Buccin : Trompette romaine légèrement recourbée.

Concursu ! : Pas de charge !

Consul : Détenteur d'une magistrature annuelle, la plus haute de la république romaine, il lève les troupes et commande l'armée avec le droit de vie et de mort sur les hommes. Il est acclamé comme *imperator* en cas de victoire.

Éclisses (ou attelles) : Plaques de bois qu'on applique sur un membre fracturé pour maintenir les os.

Hastati : Fantassins de première ligne, armés du pilum.

Laniste : Directeur d'une école de gladiateurs.

Lardoire : Tige creuse en métal servant à larder la viande.

Laticlave : Bande de pourpre appliquée verticalement sur le devant de la tunique portée par les sénateurs. Par extension, désigne le dignitaire qui porte cet insigne.

Latifundium : Grande propriété, concédée sur le domaine public, exploitée par des esclaves et vouée à la culture extensive.

Légat : Représentant de Rome auprès d'un pays étranger.

Licteur : Officier public, portant les faisceaux, chargé d'escorter les hauts magistrats.

Mango (pluriel : *mangones*) : Marchand d'esclaves.

Odin : Dieu de la guerre chez les Germains.

Optio : Sous-officier qui servait d'adjudant aux légionnaires romains.

Palus : Pieu pivotant utilisé pour l'entraînement des gladiateurs.

Pectoral : Partie de l'armure d'un légionnaire protégeant le torse.

Pilum : Javelot.

Préteur : Dignitaire chargé de la justice civile et criminelle.

Principes : Fantassins de deuxième ligne.

Proconsul : Gouverneur civil et militaire.

Procurateur : Fonctionnaire chargé de l'administration d'une province romaine.

Questeur : Magistrat chargé de la gestion financière.

Quintenaire : Soldat éclaireur.

Rétiaire : Gladiateur armé d'un filet et d'un trident.

Teutatès : Dieu de la guerre chez les Gaulois.

Torchère : Grand chandelier.

Triarii : Vétérans combattant en dernière ligne, la plus solide, dans l'armée romaine.

Tribun : Officier supérieur dépendant directement du consul.

Vélite : Soldat d'infanterie légère, armé d'un bouclier et de javelots.

Voie Appia (ou voie Appienne) : Route romaine conduisant de Rome à Brindes, l'actuelle Brindisi.

Walhalla : Paradis des guerriers dans la religion germanique et scandinave.

Pour en savoir plus

Jean-Paul Brisson, *Spartacus*, Club français du livre, 1959.
Catherine Salles, « Spartacus et la guerre des gladiateurs », revue *L'Histoire*, n° 110.
Joël Schmidt, *Vie et mort des esclaves dans la Rome antique*, Albin Michel, 2003.

Imprimé en Italie

Tu as aimé ce livre ?

Découvre les aventures d'un autre héros de légende !